First published in the United States of America in 2014 by
Chronicle Books LLC.
Originally published in Switzerland in 2013 under the title *Dada*, by
Editions La Joie de lire SA, 5 chemin Neuf, 1207 Genève-Switzerland.

Copyright © 2013 by Editions La Joie de lire SA.
Text by Germano Zullo.
Illustrations by Albertine.
English translation copyright © 2014 by Chronicle Books LLC.

Library of Congress Cataloging-in-Publication data available.

ISBN 978-1-4521-3152-8

Manufactured in China.

English translation by Taylor Norman.
Design by Amy Yu Gray.
Typeset in Bodoni Egyptian.

10 9 8 7 6 5 4 3 2 1

Chronicle Books LLC
680 Second Street
San Francisco, California 94107

Chronicle Books—we see things differently.
Become part of our community at www.chroniclekids.com.

JUMPING JACK

GERMANO ZULLO   ALBERTINE

chronicle books · san francisco

Jumping Jack and Roger Trotter were show-jumping champions. They were a perfect pair, practically invincible. You could almost say that Jack and Roger were two halves of the same person. Or two halves of the same horse. Or something.

Every year, the International Tournament of Primrose drew huge crowds. Jumping Jack and Roger Trotter were so talented that people came from all over the world to witness their glorious feats.

But, wait—was this *really* the famous
Jumping Jack and Roger Trotter?

What was happening?

They looked like
amateurs . . .

. . . and very *bad*
amateurs at that!

Such a disappointment!

Roger Trotter was worried. Very worried. Jumping Jack seemed to have lost his way. "We *must* figure out the cause of this terrible embarrassment," Roger thought. There wasn't anything else to do but consult a veterinarian.

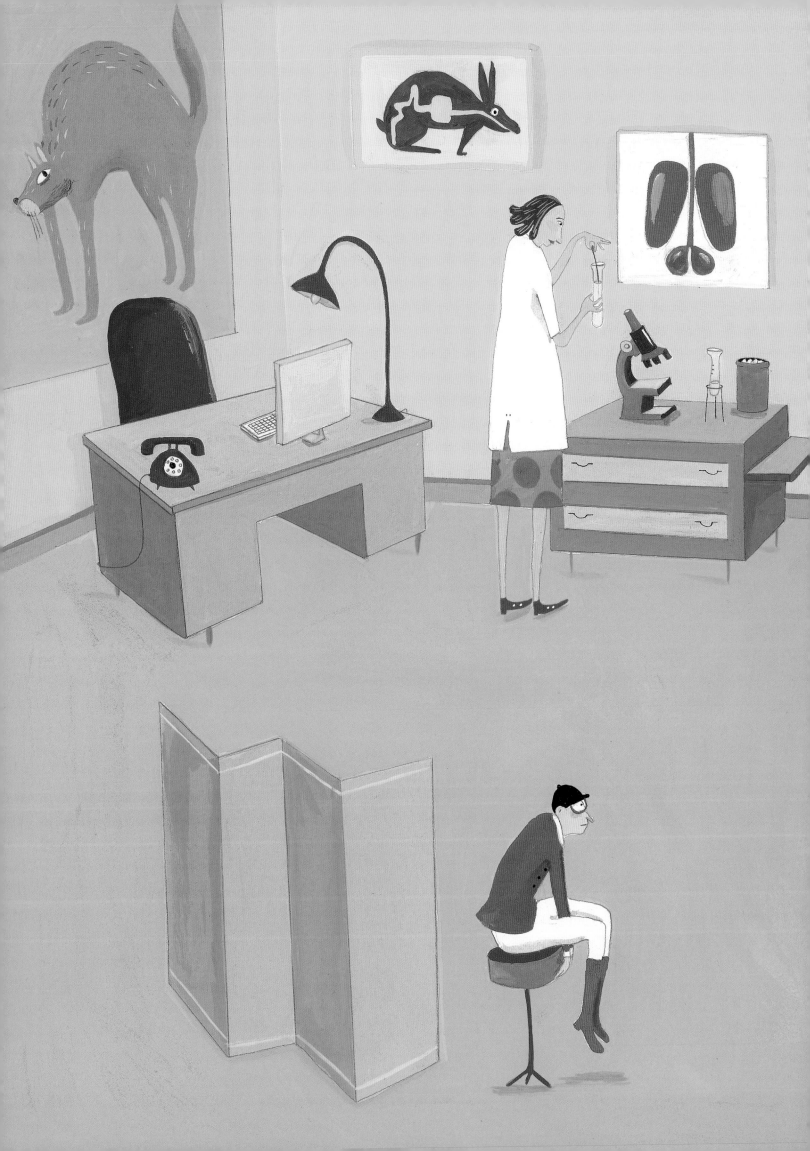

Poor Jumping Jack!

What if it was serious?

Jumping Jack was suffering from minor tendinitis in his front left hoof, a slightly contracted muscle in the buttocks, a bruised right hind hock, neuralgia in the neck, flatulence, the hint of a cavity, and an allergy to cat hair.

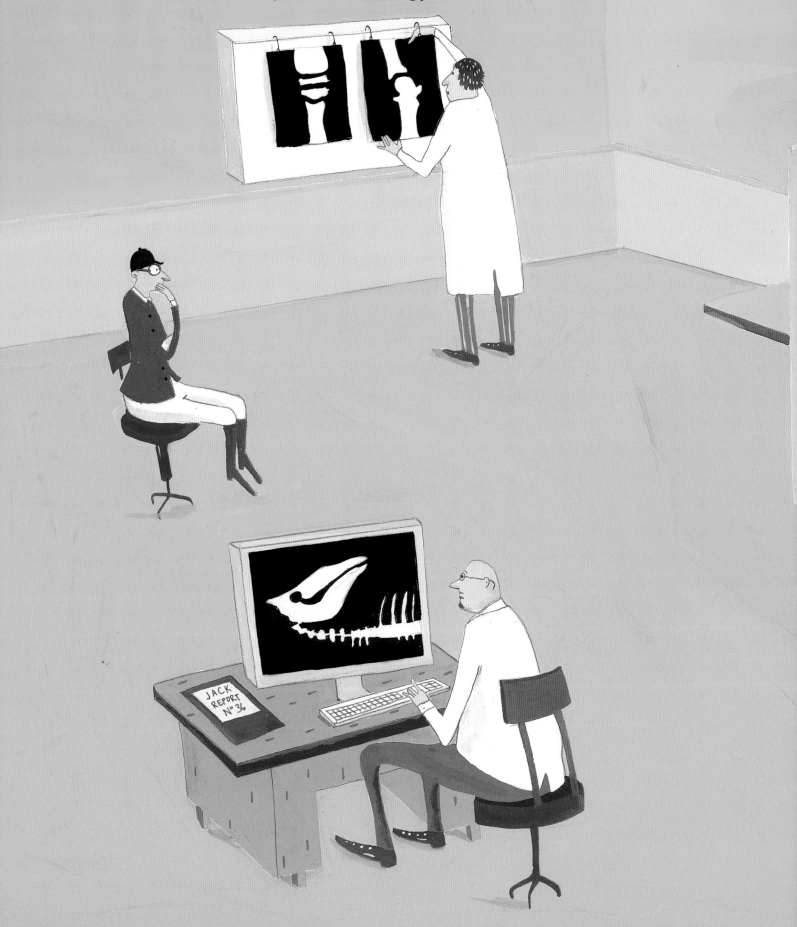

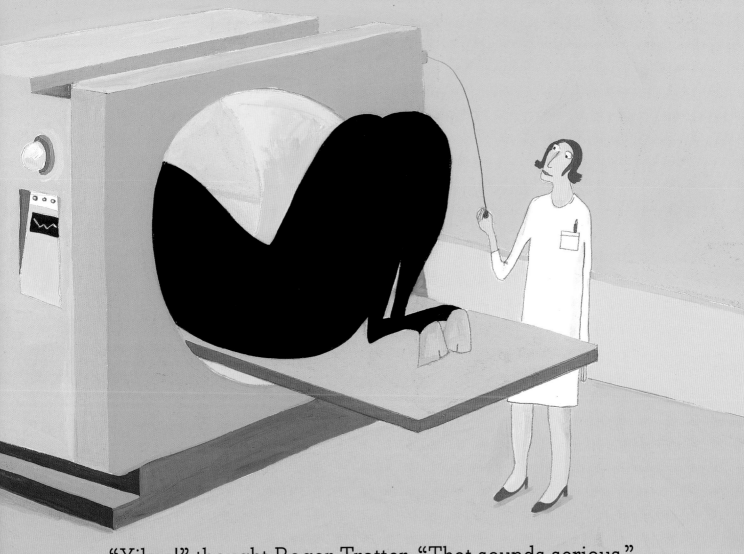

"Yikes!" thought Roger Trotter. "That sounds serious."

"It isn't serious," said the vet. "Mere boo-boos. Jumping Jack is a strong horse. None of these things should be causing him problems on the course."

The veterinarian gave Jumping Jack some vitamins and sent him on his way.

"Perhaps Jack has simply lost faith in his abilities," Roger thought. After all, it wasn't easy to be a celebrity. There wasn't anything else to do but consult a psychologist.

But the psychologist concluded that Jumping Jack was just a little bit sad, a teeny bit anxious, a tiny bit nervous, a wee bit cranky, and, of course, quite tired. "That's nothing unusual," thought Roger Trotter. The psychologist agreed. He prescribed nothing but rest.

"Surely, two weeks' vacation will return Jumping Jack to his old self!" thought Roger Trotter. Even better, two weeks in the sun would make Jack's coat sparkle and his mane silky.

The International Tournament of Martingale was the most important competition of the year. Roger Trotter was nervous. Very nervous. He whispered some final words of advice to Jumping Jack, "Control your breathing; stay relaxed; move with grace; keep your eyes on the next jump; and, of course, don't forget . . ."

"... we are champions!"

The round started off quite badly.

But then something strange happened.

Jumping Jack and Roger Trotter invented a new style—and a very *stylish* style at that!

They finished the competition brilliantly.

"Hooray!" The fans were relieved. Their favorite champions were back! Some said Jumping Jack and Roger Trotter were so good that they should be inducted into the Hall of Fame immediately.

The ophthalmologist didn't know yet if Jumping Jack was nearsighted, farsighted, or just plain cross-eyed, but one thing was certain: Jumping Jack needed glasses! Why hadn't anyone thought of this sooner?

Jumping Jack and Roger Trotter were show-jumping champions. They were a perfect pair, practically invincible. You could almost say that Jack and Roger made up two halves of the same person. Or two halves of the same horse. Or one winning team.